D1014315

WELCOME TO
PASSPORT TO READING
A beginning reader's ticket to a brand-new world!

Every book in this program is designed to build read-along and read-alone skills, level by level, through engaging and enriching stories. As the reader turns each page, he or she will become more confident with new vocabulary, sight words, and comprehension.

These PASSPORT TO READING levels will help you choose the perfect book for every reader.

READING TOGETHER
Read short words in simple sentence structures together to begin a reader's journey.

READING OUT LOUD
Encourage developing readers to sound out words in more complex stories with simple vocabulary.

READING INDEPENDENTLY
Newly independent readers gain confidence reading more complex sentences with higher word counts.

READY TO READ MORE
Readers prepare for chapter books with fewer illustrations and longer paragraphs.

This book features sight words from the educator-supported Dolch Sight Words List. This encourages the reader to recognize commonly used vocabulary words, increasing reading speed and fluency.

For more information, please visit passporttoreadingbooks.com.

Enjoy the journey!

Little, Brown and Company
Hachette Book Group
1290 Avenue of the Americas, New York, NY 10104
Visit us at LBYR.com
mylittlepony.com

First Edition: October 2018

Little, Brown and Company is a division of Hachette Book Group, Inc.
The Little, Brown name and logo are trademarks of Hachette Book Group, Inc.

The publisher is not responsible for websites (or their content) that are not owned by the publisher.

Library of Congress Control Number 2018940699

ISBNs: 978-0-316-41345-9 (pbk.), 978-0-316-41347-3 (ebook), 978-0-316-41348-0 (ebook), 978-0-316-41346-6 (ebook)

Printed in the United States of America

CW

10 9 8 7 6 5 4 3 2 1

Passport to Reading titles are leveled by independent reviewers applying the standards developed by Irene Fountas and Gay Su Pinnell in *Matching Books to Readers: Using Leveled Books in Guided Reading*, Heinemann, 1999.

Licensed By:

Meet the
New Class

by Jennifer Fox

LITTLE, BROWN AND COMPANY
New York   Boston

Attention, My Little Pony fans!

Look for these words when you read this book.

Can you spot them all?

Yak

laugh

classmates

book

Princess Twilight Sparkle
makes her dream come true.
She opens a School of Friendship.

A school needs teachers.
And Twilight has just
the right crew...

...her friends Rainbow Dash, Fluttershy, Applejack, Pinkie Pie, and Rarity! Starlight Glimmer and Spike will help, too.

The school is not just for ponies.
"Friendship should be shared
with everycreature!"
says Twilight.

Her new students come from
all kinds of kingdoms in Equestria
and beyond!

Yona is a sturdy young Yak
from Yakyakistan.
Like most Yaks,
Yona says that "Yak is best."

Smolder is a fiery little Dragon.
She is a bit of a know-it-all,
and she loves to win.

Ocellus is a very shy Changeling.
To fit in with new friends,
she matches their shapes.

Silverstream is one
hyped-up Hippogriff!
She is always ready to fly off
and find some fun.

Sandbar is a cool pony.

He has a warm, beachy vibe.

He likes to keep the peace

and does not make waves.

Gallus is a Griffin with
lots of attitude.
He learned from the best:
his grumpy Grampa Gruff.

The students in Twilight's
new school are all so different!

At first, it is hard

for them to get along.

Soon, they try new things...
together.

The students start to have
some fun…

...and they share a few laughs.

"Yona like new friends!"

The students work hard
and play hard.

They learn to work as a team
and build trust.

The new class is there
for one another
when there is trouble.

"Puckwudgie attack!"

They even cause
a bit of trouble themselves!

The classmates learn
that not every lesson
can be found in a book.

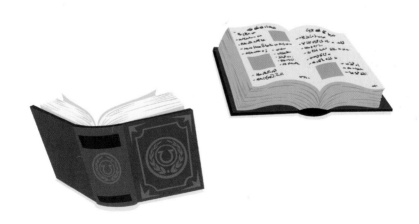

And they learn that good friends
can be the best teachers of all!